ROSE AND DOROTHY

KIDS CAN PRESS LTD.

TORONTO

ROSE AND DOROTHY

WRITTEN AND ILLUSTRATED BY Roslyn Schwartz

Kids Can Press Ltd. acknowledges with appreci-
ation the assistance of the Canada Council and
the Ontario Arts Council in the production of
this book.

Canadian Cataloguing in Publication Data

Schwartz, Roslyn
  Rose and Dorothy

ISBN 0-921103-93-X (bound) ISBN 1-55074-065-2 (pbk.)

I. Title.

PS8587.C58R68 1990   jC813′.54   C89-090559-2
PZ7.S33Ro 1990

Kids Can Press Ltd.,
585½ Bloor Street West,
Toronto, Ontario, Canada, M6G 1K5.

Book design by Michael Solomon
Printed and bound in Hong Kong

PA 92 0 9 8 7 6 5 4 3 2 1

Rose lived all by herself in a house with too many rooms.

Then she met Dorothy and invited her to move in.

Dorothy was larger than life to Rose and twice as charming.

They went shopping together.

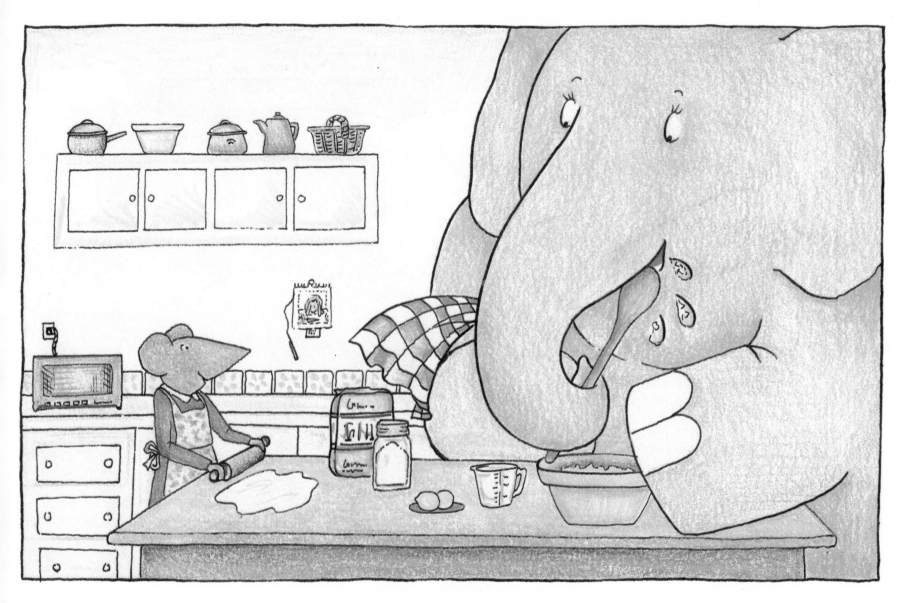

And cooked together.

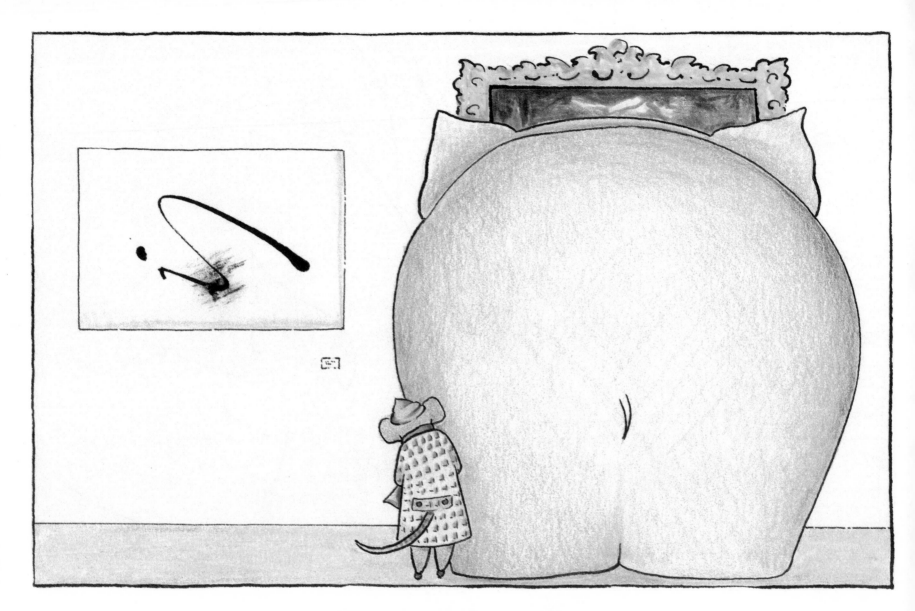

They went to the art gallery.

And entertained often.

Dorothy liked to sing.

They even went on holiday together.
(Dorothy seemed to tan faster than Rose.)

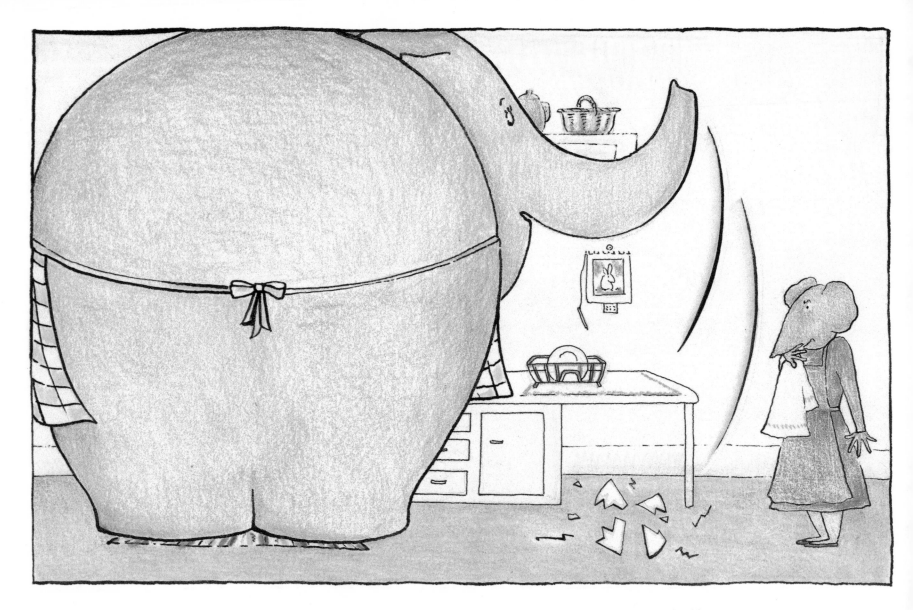

Then one day, Rose thought: "How clumsy she is."

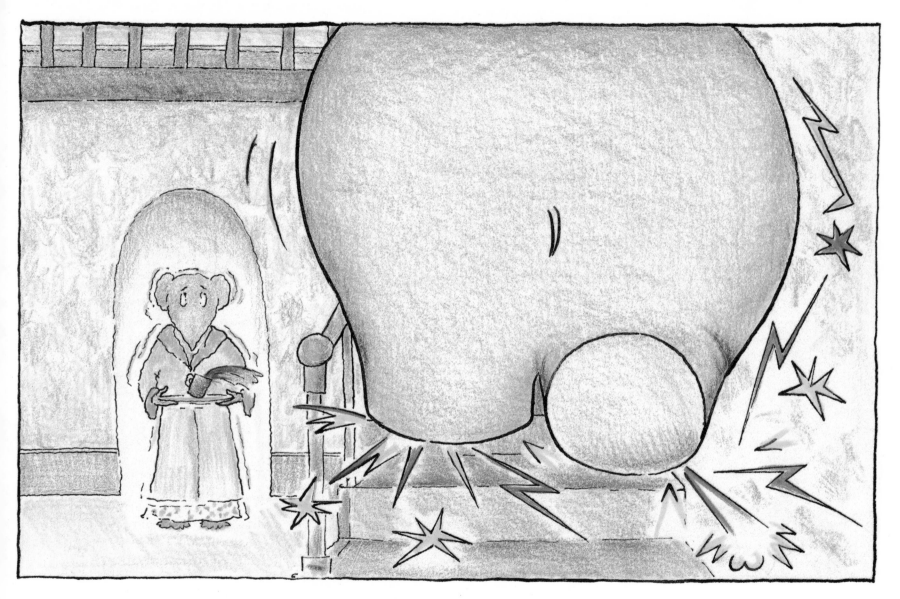

And how noisy!

And how messy!

Rose took to her room.

Then to her bed.

Finally, she fled next door.

Her neighbour, Alice, was most kind. . .

and poured tea from a pot with two spouts.

Rose talked and talked. Alice listened.

So did Dorothy.

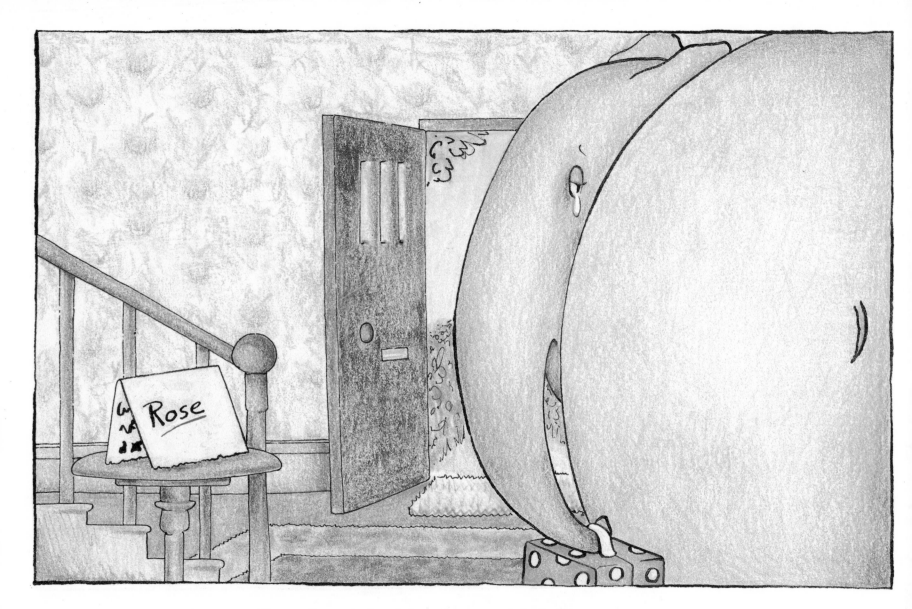

Dorothy packed her bag and left Rose a note.

Lost, tired and hungry, she could go no further.

"Oooowoooh!" she wailed. "What will I do?
I can't stay here forever."

"I'll have to get a job."

Dorothy was an overnight success.

Rose was wretched.

She called Dorothy. They talked and talked.

Dorothy bought the big house next to Rose and Alice.

They saw each other often and were friends for life.